This LADYBIRD TALE
belongs to

....

The Elves and the Shoemaker

Retold by Vera Southgate M.A., B.COM
with illustrations by Sarah Preston

LADYBIRD TALES

ONCE UPON A TIME there lived a shoemaker and his wife.

The man was a good shoemaker and he worked hard, yet he and his wife were very poor.

As time went on, they grew poorer and poorer.

At last the day came when all the shoemaker had left was one piece of leather. It would make only one pair of shoes.

That evening, before he went to bed, the shoemaker cut out a pair of shoes from the leather. Then he left them on his workbench all ready for him to sew the next morning.

As they were going upstairs to bed that night, the shoemaker spoke sadly to his wife.

"I have used my last piece of leather," he said. "I have cut out one pair of shoes. Tomorrow I will sew them. When they are sold, I do not know what will become of us."

The next morning, the shoemaker got up early and went into his workshop, ready to make the shoes.

On his bench, instead of the leather he had left cut out, he found a pair of shoes, already made.

He was astonished and did not know what to think.

The shoemaker took the shoes in his hands and looked carefully at them. They were neatly made, with not one bad stitch in them.

He showed the shoes to his wife who said, "I have never seen a pair of shoes so well made. They are perfect."

The shoemaker and his wife could not think who had sewn the shoes.

The same morning, a lady came into the shop to buy a pair of shoes.

The shoemaker showed her the pair he had found on his bench. She said, "I have never seen such well-made shoes."

The lady tried on the shoes and they fitted her perfectly. She was so pleased with them that she paid the shoemaker twice the usual price.

With the money, the shoemaker was able to buy leather for two more pairs of shoes.

That night, before he went to bed, he cut out two pairs of shoes from the leather. He left them on his workbench all ready to sew the next morning.

The next morning, the shoemaker got up early and went into his shop to make the shoes. But he had no need to do so. On his bench he found two pairs of shoes, already made.

He took the shoes in his hands and looked carefully at them. Once more he found that they were neatly made, with not one bad stitch in them.

That morning, a man came into the shop to buy some shoes.

The shoemaker showed him the two pairs of shoes he had found on his bench. The man said, "I have never seen such well-made shoes."

He was so pleased with them that he bought both pairs of shoes and paid the shoemaker twice the usual price.

And so it went on. Every night, the shoemaker cut out some leather and left it on his workbench.

Every morning, he found the shoes all neatly made.

Many rich customers came to his shop to buy these perfect shoes. So, in time, the shoemaker and his wife became rich.

One evening, not long before Christmas, when the shoemaker had finished cutting out shoes, he went to his wife.

"We still do not know who sews the shoes for us," he said. "Shall we stay up tonight to see who it is that helps us?"

His wife thought that this was a very good idea. So she lit a candle and they went into the workshop.

They hid themselves in a corner of the room.

Then the shoemaker and his wife waited quietly and watched to see what would happen.

For a long time nothing happened. Then, just as the clock struck midnight, the door of the workshop opened quietly.

In came two tiny elves. They were dressed in old clothes and their feet were bare.

They did not see the shoemaker and his wife, who were hiding in the corner, watching them.

The elves jumped onto the workbench and took up the shoes that were cut out. They began to stitch and sew and hammer. They worked so neatly and so quickly that the shoemaker could hardly believe his eyes.

The elves did not stop for a moment until all the cut-out shoes were finished. Then they ran quickly away.

The next morning, at breakfast,
the shoemaker asked his wife,
"How can we thank these little
elves, who have made us so rich
and so happy?"

"I know what we can do," said
his wife. "We can make them new
clothes and shoes. Their own
clothes are ragged and their feet
are bare."

During the evenings that followed, the shoemaker and his wife began to make new clothes for the elves.

The shoemaker chose the softest leather he could find. He cut out two of the tiniest pairs of shoes ever seen. Then he stitched the shoes as carefully as he could.

The shoemaker's wife cut out two white shirts, two small green jackets and two pairs of trousers to match. She sewed them with tiny stitches.

She made two little caps, each with a feather in it.

She also knitted two pairs of tiny white stockings.

By Christmas Eve, the tiny shoes and clothes were finished.

The shoemaker cleared the leather and the tools from his workbench. He and his wife laid their presents on the bench, instead of the usual work.

Then they hid themselves, as they had done before, and waited to see what the elves would do.

Just as the clock struck midnight, the door opened quietly, as before. The two elves came running in. They still wore old clothes and their feet were blue with cold.

They jumped onto the bench, ready to get to work at once. But there was no leather on the bench, only the tiny clothes.

The elves were astonished at first, and then they were delighted. In no time at all, they were out of their old clothes.

Then they dressed themselves in the beautiful new clothes – the green jackets and trousers, the white shirts and stockings, the soft leather shoes and little caps, with the feathers that nodded as they laughed.

Then they joined hands and danced around, singing,

*"Now we are boys so fine to see,
We need no longer cobblers be."*

At last they danced happily out of the door.

The shoemaker and his wife never saw the little elves again. But, from that time, good luck was always with them.

They were rich and happy for the rest of their lives.

A History of
The Elves and the Shoemaker

The Elves and the Shoemaker has inspired a number of film and cartoon characters, including Dobby the house-elf in *Harry Potter and the Chamber of Secrets.*

The original story of *The Elves and the Shoemaker* appeared as one of three tales known as *Die Wichtelmänner*, written by the Brothers Grimm in 1812. Later, these stories were translated into English by Margaret Hunt and became known as *The Elves.*

There have been a number of variations since the original story first appeared. In one version, the shoemaker uses the money he makes from the sale of the first pair of shoes to pay his rent and to buy food before buying more leather. Other versions refer to him giving money to the poor or giving shoes to the needy.

Ladybird's classic retelling from 1965, written by Vera Southgate, brought this much-loved tale to a new generation of readers.

Collect more fantastic

LADYBIRD  TALES

Little Red
Riding Hood

9781409311126

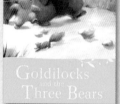

Goldilocks
and the
Three Bears

9781409311119

Cinderella

9781409311072

Jack
and the
Beanstalk

9781409311102

The
Gingerbread
Man

9781409311096

The Three
Little Pigs

9781409311089

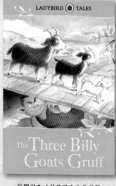

The Three Billy
Goats Gruff

9781409311065

Hansel
and
Gretel

9781409311133

to buy food before buying more leather. Other versions refer to him giving money to the poor or giving shoes to the needy.

Ladybird's classic retelling from 1965, written by Vera Southgate, brought this much-loved tale to a new generation of readers.

Collect more fantastic
LADYBIRD 🐞 TALES

Little Red
Riding Hood

9781409311126

Goldilocks
and the
Three Bears

9781409311119

Cinderella

9781409311072

Jack
and the
Beanstalk

9781409311102

The
Gingerbread
Man

9781409311096

The Three
Little Pigs

9781409311089

The Three Billy
Goats Gruff

9781409311065

Hansel
and
Gretel

9781409311133

Puss in Boots
9781409311225

Rapunzel
9781409311195

Rumpelstiltskin
9781409311164

The Elves and the Shoemaker
9781409311188

Snow White and the Seven Dwarfs
9781409311171

The Enormous Turnip
9781409311218

The Magic Porridge Pot
9781409311201

Sleeping Beauty
9781409311157

Endpapers taken from series 606d,
first published in 1964

A catalogue record for this book is available from the British Library

Published by Ladybird Books Ltd
80 Strand London WC2R 0RL
A Penguin Company

001 – 10 9 8 7 6 5 4 3 2 1

ISBN: 978-1-40931-118-8

Printed in China